To my parents

Pauline would like to thank Annebeth Suter,
Paul Flora, Gertraud Middelhauve, Anne
de Bouchony, and Christine Baker, as well
as Kate, Laura, and especially Anne.

Library of Congress Cataloging-in-Publication Data
Hallensleben, Georg.
    Pauline / Georg Hallensleben.
      p. cm.
    1st ed.
    "Frances Foster books."
    SUMMARY: Pauline the weasel has an imaginative plan to rescue
her elephant friend who has been trapped by hunters.
    ISBN 0-374-35758-7
    I. Title.
PZ7.H15425Pau 1999
[E]—dc21   98-8054

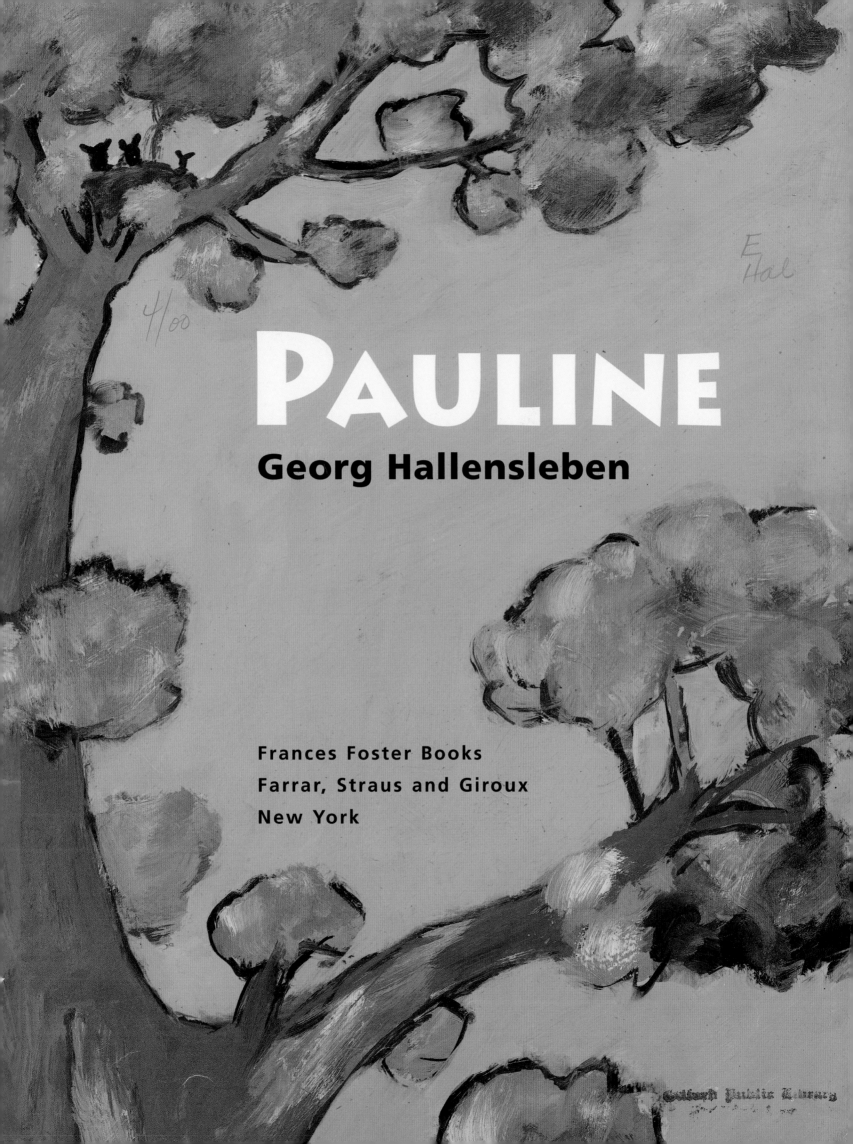

PAULINE

Georg Hallensleben

Frances Foster Books
Farrar, Straus and Giroux
New York

In the branches of a tall tree lived a pair of fuzzy-eared weasels with their daughter, Pauline.

From her perch high in the sky, Pauline would look down at the jungle and see, far below on the ground, small animals moving around.

"When can I go down there?" she would ask.

"When you're bigger," her parents would say.

Then one day Pauline was big enough to go out on her own.
As she stood in the middle of the jungle, she couldn't believe
her eyes.
There were vines that leaped from the trees, and colorful
flowers.
And the small animals she had seen from the tree were
much bigger than she was.

Suddenly it grew dark.
Something gray and enormous walked right over her.
"Help!" shrieked Pauline.
"Excuse me," came a voice from above. "Why, I thought you
were a stone. Don't be afraid. I'm only an elephant, and a little
one at that. My name is Rabusius. But who are you?"
Rabusius had to listen very carefully to hear the tiny voice that
answered. "I'm Pauline."

Rabusius and Pauline became inseparable.
They swam together in the lake.
They played hide-and-seek.
And sometimes Pauline let him win.
"Where are you, Rabusius?"

Then, one terrible day, four hunters came along.
They pounced on Rabusius and trapped him in a net,
while Pauline watched helplessly.
"I will save you!" cried Pauline.
But she didn't know how.
"Let's get this monster inside the truck," she heard one
of the hunters say.
"How could they call him a monster?" thought Pauline.
And then she had an idea.

She ran home to her parents and explained her plan.
They set to work with feathers, paints, and a white
mask, and in no time at all Pauline had turned into
a frightening monster.

Nobody recognized her as she raced through the jungle.
She jumped from tree to tree, hoping to reach the truck in time.

Rabusius was tied up inside the truck. He felt lost and terribly afraid.

Pauline climbed into the old palm tree by the bridge and hid among its branches. She could see the truck coming closer.

And when the truck crossed the bridge she waved
her long arms with all her might.
"Help! A monster!" shouted the hunters.

Pauline jumped on top of the truck and hung upside down in front of the big windshield, looking right into the driver's eyes.

The frightened driver trembled and the truck swerved to the left, then to the right, and then went straight into the ditch. The hunters jumped out of the truck and ran for their lives.

Pauline opened the big doors.
When Rabusius saw her, he shrieked.
"Don't be afraid," said Pauline. "I'm only a little
monster, and a friendly one at that. It's me, Pauline."

The next day, the whole jungle knew what Pauline had done. She and Rabusius threw an enormous party for all their friends and relatives. Everyone came dressed as a monster and they sang and danced the night away.